LUCIE
GOOSE

DANNY BAKER

Illustrated by
PIPPA CURNICK

Hodder
Children's
Books

Lucie Goose lived all alone in a house on the very edge of the woods. As far as she could remember, she had always lived by herself and had never met or spoken to another animal of any sort.

One day, and I think it was a Tuesday,
Lucie was in her garden watering the carrot patch
when out of a dark clump of trees came a wolf.
He tiptoed right up to Lucie and said,

"I'm sorry," said Lucie.
"What did you say?"

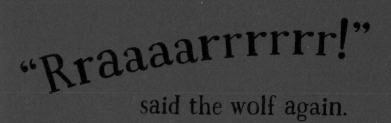

"Rraaaarrrrrr!"
said the wolf again.

"Rraaaarrrrrr?"
said Lucie, puzzled.
"What's
'Rraaaarrrrrr'?"

"Well, just rraaaarrrrrr,"
answered the wolf.
"You run away and
I chase after you.
But I go rraaarrr first."

"Don't be silly," said Lucie with a little laugh. "I'm not doing that. You seem very nice – like a big woolly sausage. Perhaps you'd like to come inside for a cup of tea and a piece of cake?"

"No, no, no!" grumbled the wolf, turning around and stomping back into the woods.

"I can't eat cake with a goose!
Oh, this is not what's supposed to happen at all!"

And then
he was gone.

Lucie thought about the
wolf for a little while,
but soon moved on
to the very important
business of picking
strawberries.

Just then, from out
of the dark clump
of trees, came an
enormous bear…

"I beg your pardon?" said Lucie Goose.

"Rorioorrrr!"

repeated the bear, this time with some extra nail-waggling.

"I see," said Lucie. "I'm sorry, I'm not very good at being scared."

"Right, I'll rorioorrrr again and you can scream and run away, yes?" suggested the bear.

"No, thank you," said Lucie Goose.
"You seem very nice too – like a comfy winter coat.
You're quite welcome to come inside
for tea and cake if you like?"

"No, no, no!" wailed the big bear, turning around and stomping back into the woods. "I can't sit and drink tea with a goose! Oh, this is not what's supposed to happen at all!"

And then
he was gone.

Lucie thought about the
bear for a little while.
She even thought about
the wolf. But before long
she had moved on to the
very important business
of picking some flowers.

Just then, out of the dark clump of trees,
came a lion, shaking his head and making a
very cross-looking face at the same time...

"Oh no,"
said Lucie Goose,
"not another one."

The lion couldn't
remember anybody **NOT**
running away screaming
from one of his best
roars before.

"It's all right, I know what you want," said Lucie.
"You go rrrrooooaaar, I run away and you chase after me.
But I'm **NOT** scared."

"Everyone runs from
lions," said the lion.
"Now then, shall I roar
again and we start
from the beginning?"

"I'm sorry, lion," said Lucie Goose, trying to be helpful. "You're the first lion I've ever met and you look very nice – like a fat old carpet. Why don't you come inside and have some tea and cake?"

"No, no, no!" thundered the lion, turning around and stomping back into the woods. "I can't sit having tea and cake with a goose. Oh, this isn't what's supposed to happen at all!"

And then
he was gone.

Lucie thought about the lion for a while. She thought
a little bit about the wolf and the big bear as well.
Why, she wondered, was everyone always trying
to scare everybody else?

Just then, out of the dark clump
of trees came a goose.

"Goodness me," said Lucie, "you're not going to shout **rraaar** or **rorioorrr** or **rroooaaarrr** at me as well, are you?"

"Erm, not really," said Bruce nervously. "You see, I'm just a goose, the same as you. Bruce Goose. And nobody is really scared of us gooses."

"Well, that's a relief!" said Lucie.
"Come inside and have a cup of tea
and some cake. Or do you think
that's not how things are supposed to be?"

"I'd love some tea and cake,"
said Bruce, smiling.

Bruce followed Lucie along the pretty little path lined
with lupins and over the gurgling stream that hurried its
way across a bed of wonderfully coloured stones.

Passing under an archway made of jasmine flowers,
they arrived at the front of the house...

. . . and just then, something ran past them as fast as a flash.

It was the bear.

Then something ran past them as fast as a plane.

It was the wolf.

Then something ran past them as fast as a lion.

It was the lion.

They all ran into Lucie's house.

"Have you changed your minds?" said Lucie happily,
but a tiny bit puzzled.
"Yes," said the wolf. "I remembered I like tea!"
"Absolutely," said the bear and the lion. "We adore cake."

"How marvellous!" beamed Lucie. "Please stay as long as you like."
"Oh, we will. . ." said her new friends. "We will. . ."

Written for and many times told to my eternal toddlers:
Bonnie, Sonny & Mancie (Bon Bon, Matey & Moo!) – D.B.

To Jaw & Dard, Marion & Ian: Chief Babysitters
And to Roux: Chief Baby – P.C.

HODDER CHILDREN'S BOOKS

First published in Great Britain in 2017 by Hodder and Stoughton
This edition published in 2017

A CIP catalogue record for this book
is available from the British Library.

HB ISBN: 978 1 444 93739 8
PB ISBN: 978 1 444 93740 4

3 5 7 9 10 8 6 4 2

Printed and bound in China

MIX
Paper from
responsible sources
FSC
www.fsc.org   FSC® C104740

Hodder Children's Books
An imprint of Hachette Children's Group
Part of Hodder and Stoughton
Carmelite House
50 Victoria Embankment
London EC4Y 0DZ

An Hachette UK Company
www.hachette.co.uk

www.hachettechildrens.co.uk